A CARTOON NETWORK ORIGINAL

the POWERPUFF GIRLS

TALES FROM TOWNSVILLE

BY CANDACE BRYAN
ILLUSTRATED BY STEPHEN REED

CARTOON
NETWORK
B O O K S

AN IMPRINT OF PENGUIN RANDOM HOUSE

CARTOON NETWORK BOOKS
Penguin Young Readers Group
An Imprint of Penguin Random House LLC

TM and © Cartoon Network. (s17). All rights reserved. Published in 2017 by Cartoon Network Books, an imprint of Penguin Random House LLC, 345 Hudson Street, New York, New York 10014. Manufactured in China.

ISBN 9780451533005   10 9 8 7 6 5 4 3 2 1

BLOSSOM'S NEW JOB

"YES! YES!" Blossom cheered as the Powerpuff Girls passed by a shop window on their way home from school.

"What are we excited about?" asked Bubbles. "Did you see a cute puppy?"

"Or did someone fall in some mud?" added Buttercup.

Blossom pointed to the window. "That!" she said.

Hanging in the window was a display of new shiny red backpacks.

"Is there a bad guy hiding in that backpack?" asked Bubbles.

"A bad guy!" Buttercup yelled. "Let me at him."

"Wait," said Blossom, blocking her sister. "Look. At. That. Backpack. It's the new Ultimate Superstar Backpack. I just read about it in *Weekly Backpack Magazine*. I have to have it."

"What's wrong with the backpack you have now?" Buttercup asked Blossom, pointing to her very large and practical bag. "It's just a place to keep all your crud while you're at school."

"Yeah," chimed in Bubbles. "We all have the same backpack, just different colors. I love mine. I even put a kitten sticker on it. I can put one on yours, if you want."

"You don't understand," Blossom said with a huff. "I *need* a new Ultimate Superstar Backpack so I can carry home all my textbooks every day and study even harder. Plus, I really want to be able to keep all my pens organized. Without that backpack, how can

I possibly stay on top of all my classes?"

Blossom zipped into the store and straight to the shiny red backpack. She pulled it from its display case and tried it on. As soon as the straps hit her shoulders, a huge grin spread across her face and she flew around the store in ecstasy. *Just imagine how great it would be to own this*, she thought to herself.

"Look how much stuff you can fit in it!" she shouted gleefully to her sisters. "You can fit over A HUNDRED PENS in this one pocket alone!"

Her sisters were not impressed.

A teenaged salesperson shook his head as he watched Blossom running and flying around. "Um, if you're, like, not going to buy this backpack, you need to put it back, okay?" he said.

Blossom's heart sank and she reluctantly peeled the bag off her back.

"I don't have any money," she said, and walked out of the store with a heavy head and droopy bow.

"Why don't you ask the Professor to buy it for you?" asked Bubbles.

"It was just our birthday," Blossom replied. "He said no new presents for a while."

Just then, something totally amazing happened.

On a store across the street hung the most beautiful, shining sign that Blossom had ever seen.

It said: **WANT TO MAKE MONEY? COME WORK FOR US! WE ARE HIRING!**

Blossom's eyes doubled in size, and her red bow perked up. The gears in her brain started to turn.

"If I get a job, I can earn my own money and save up to buy the Ultimate Superstar Backpack myself!" she shrieked in excitement.

"Dude, how can you get a job when you have to go to school every day?" Buttercup asked.

"Are people our age even allowed to get jobs?" Bubbles wondered out loud.

"Guys, come on!" Blossom replied. "I can work after school. Or before school. Or on the weekends. Plus, it will only be for a little while so I can save up for the Backpack. Of. My. Dreams!"

Before Buttercup or Bubbles could respond, Blossom dashed into the store.

Inside, Blossom saw piles of clothes lying around all over the place. Everything in the store was black and sleek.

"Welcome to B&B Fashion!" a voice boomed. Blossom looked around, but didn't see anyone. "Welcome!" the voice repeated. The voice seemed to be coming out of a small black speaker near the back.

"Hi, my name is Blossom," the Powerpuff Girl yelled. She wasn't sure who she was talking to, or if anyone could hear her. "I am very smart, I'm a very hard worker, and I want this job more than anything else in the whole wide world. Oh please oh please oh please let me work for you!"

"You're hired!" the voice shouted without hesitation. "Your first day of work will be tomorrow. Don't be late!"

Blossom walked out of the store grinning and shared her news with Bubbles and Buttercup. "Told you I could get a job," she said.

The two sisters still thought it was a bad idea, though,

and Blossom didn't tell them that her new workplace was more than a little creepy.

After school the next day, Blossom rushed straight to B&B Fashion. When she arrived at her new workplace, the mysterious voice from the speaker put Blossom to work, giving her all the directions she needed to do her job.

"Fold these clothes, hang up those clothes, make flyers, help the shoppers, sweep the floor, clean the dressing room." The list of tasks seemed like it would never end. "And don't forget to hang the 'Sale' sign in the window." As soon as the sign went up, the shop filled with customers, and Blossom got even busier.

The next day at work, the number of customers had doubled. Blossom was surprised that the boring black clothes were so popular. Then a customer accidentally dropped a magazine on the floor. Blossom picked it up and read the cover. It said "Don't Be Weird: How to Look Stylish and Fit in with the Crowd." The story inside explained how to tell what was tacky and what was not, and why everyone needed to dress in the new Townsville trend: all black. Next to the story was a full-page advertisement telling Townsville readers to go shopping at B&B Fashion. Blossom's eyes grew wide as she read.

Much later that night, Blossom came home. Buttercup and Bubbles were still up playing video games. Their jaws dropped when they saw Blossom. She was dressed in all black from head to toe, including her signature bow. Her eyes were lifeless.

"Uh, Blossom, why are you dressed like that?" Buttercup asked. Blossom looked straight ahead, not at Buttercup, and answered her sister in a strange, monotonous voice.

"I got a makeover for work. This is our new

uniform. Now I and the rest of Townsville will be stylish."

"Since when do you care about fashion?" Bubbles asked.

"Looking fashionable is the most important thing a person can do. At B&B Fashion, we're trying to transform TACKY TOWNSVILLE into the chic city it should be."

The next day after school, Buttercup and Bubbles followed Blossom to the store. On their way, the two girls noticed something very unusual. Everyone in Townsville was wearing black.

There was a long line of people waiting to get inside B&B Fashion. They were all talking about the same thing: B&B Fashion's newest line.

"The new Townsville look is so chic," said one person.

"I'm *burning* all my old clothes," said another.

"Anyone not wearing these clothes is so tacky," said a

third, as they all eyed Bubbles's and Buttercup's bright blue and green dresses.

"Why are people so excited about this clothing?" Buttercup asked. "It's all so boring and black. And since when did the citizens of Townsville start caring about fashion so much?"

Eventually, she and Bubbles pushed their way to the front of the line, and finally got inside the store. There they found Blossom, flying around in a frenzy, selling the plain, dark garments.

"Welcome to B&B Fashion! Let me know if I can help you with anything!" said Blossom, so caught up in work that she didn't notice her sisters right in front of her.

"Dude, it's us! Buttercup and Bubbles," said Buttercup.

"Oh sorry, can't talk now, guys, I'm very busy," Blossom replied as she zipped away.

"When is your break?" Bubbles called after her. "We can talk to you then!"

"Break? No, I don't get a break," answered Blossom. "This is the busiest time of year, so I have to keep working until the store closes."

"What about your coworkers?" asked Buttercup. "Can't they watch the store for you to have a break?"

Blossom started laughing. "Ha! I don't have coworkers! I don't need coworkers! I've got everything under control and everything is going totally fine!"

"**HELLO!** I'M TRYING TO BUY THIS!" a man yelled from across the store, angrily waving around a black button-up shirt and glaring at Blossom.

"Sorry, got to go." Blossom dashed over to the customer and continued working.

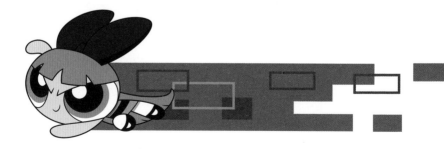

Suddenly, a voice boomed out from an intercom. "Everything is now on sale, fifty percent off!"

The line to the store, which was already around the block, immediately doubled. Some customers who had already purchased things got back in line after the announcement.

"Wait, isn't that voice kind of familiar?" asked Bubbles.

"I think I know who the voice is," Buttercup replied. "It's Bianca Bikini!"

Bianca Bikini, along with her giant apelike sister, Barbarus, was part of the notorious evil duo known as the Fashionistas. These evil sisters had tried to take over Townsville before, and their sleek all-black style was iconic. It totally explained the clothing at B&B Fashion.

"I guess it makes sense that the Fashionistas would sell clothes, but why are the people who live in Townsville wearing them and acting so weird?"

Buttercup wondered out loud. "Even Blossom is wearing their style now."

Buttercup slowly approached the suspicious black speaker. On the wall behind it were two small hinges. **A SECRET DOOR!** She motioned for Bubbles to join her, and the two sisters walked through the mysterious door down a dark hallway. At the end they found a room. Peering inside they saw Bianca and Barbarus Bikini.

"I knew it!" Buttercup yelled. Bianca Bikini turned around, laughing.

"Hello, Powerpuff Girls, we've been expecting you." She grinned and her thin eyebrows arched. A door slammed shut behind Bubbles and Buttercup. Before they could say anything, the enormous Barbarus reached out with her mammoth monkey arm, grabbed Bubbles and Buttercup, and hurled them across the room. The two Powerpuff Girls **CRASHED** against the wall. Stumbling back to their feet, Bubbles and Buttercup began to fight the evil Bikini sisters.

After a long bout of punching and kicking, though, Bubbles and Buttercup started to get tired. The Powerpuff Girls weren't as powerful without Blossom.

"Bubbles, I can take them for a few minutes. Try to open that door so we can get out of here," said Buttercup, dodging Barbarus's fist.

Bubbles flew to the door and tried to open it, but it was locked shut. She tugged at it with all her strength, but the door didn't budge.

"I have a plan," said Buttercup, and she launched a superstrong punch at Barbarus. The huge ape CRASHED against the door, cracking a hole just big enough for the girls to fit through.

The two sisters escaped quickly and flew out of the store.

"What should we do? We can't defeat both of the Bikini sisters without Blossom!" said Bubbles.

"Blossom only got this job because of the Ultimate Superstar Backpack," Buttercup replied. "Maybe if she sees it, she'll be reminded why she got this job and she'll snap back to reality."

Bubbles and Buttercup raced to the backpack store. When they got there, they saw all the Ultimate Superstar Backpacks in a pile on top of the trash can.

"Uh, we were hoping to buy one of those Ultimate Superstar Backpacks. Why are they in the garbage?" Buttercup asked.

The store employee, now dressed in all black,

laughed for a moment, but stopped when he saw the girls weren't laughing along. "Oh, you were serious? I didn't think anyone would want these *tacky* backpacks," he explained. "But if you want one, just take it. They're totally not cool this season, so they're pretty much worthless."

"Awesome!" Buttercup said, snatching a red one from the pile of discarded bags.

Back at B&B Fashion, Blossom looked exhausted. With her pale skin and black outfit, she looked like a zombie. Bubbles and Buttercup flew over to her, but she didn't even notice them.

"Blossom, it's us, your sisters, Bubbles and Buttercup!" Bubbles yelled.

"Okay, so what?" Blossom answered.

"Look what we got, Blossom," Buttercup announced, holding up the shiny red bag to Blossom's face.

"Ew, what is that tacky bag?" Blossom cringed.

"Are you kidding, Blossom? This is the Ultimate

Superstar Backpack, remember? It's the whole reason you got this job."

"Backpacks are tacky," Blossom replied. "I only carry this stylish little purse now." She held up an impossibly tiny black bag.

"But how will you fit your textbooks in that?" Bubbles asked. "How will you carry home your books to study for class?"

"Studying?" Blossom retorted sassily. "Studying is tacky. Stylish people don't care about school, we only care about fashion."

"Oh, really?" Buttercup responded. "How about this? Is this tacky?" She opened up the Ultimate Superstar Backpack and revealed its special pockets, including the one Blossom had been so excited about. Buttercup grabbed some pens out of her own pocket and put them in the backpack.

Blossom couldn't help herself. Seeing the pens organized and all the space in the backpack gave her

feelings that were so much stronger than her need to be fashionable. The black clothes peeled off and underneath was her favorite red dress. She pulled her red bow out of her pocket and snapped it back into place on her head.

"I can't believe I finally have an **ULTIMATE SUPERSTAR BACKPACK!** Ahh!" She hugged her sisters. "Thank you so much, guys!"

Suddenly confused, Blossom said, "I don't know what happened to me. I was working here, then I read this magazine about the latest fashion trend, and the next thing I knew I was wearing all black and the only thing I cared about was looking cool."

"It was the Fashionistas," Bubbles explained. "They own B&B Fashion, and have been using the power of trendy clothing to make everyone look the same."

"It made everyone act super weird," Buttercup added.

Buttercup and Bubbles led Blossom to the back room of B&B Fashion, where they found the Fashionistas planning out the next edition of their magazine.

"What tacky Townsville tradition can we do away with this month?" Bianca wondered aloud. "It's so easy to trick these simpletons into doing and wearing whatever we say. Now Townsville is no longer an eyesore, and with the money we've made, we can go on a mad shopping spree," she said, laughing. Barbarus nodded vigorously in agreement.

"Not so fast," Blossom interrupted, causing both of the Bikini sisters to jump in surprise. "You two may know a bit about fashion, but your rule over Townsville is officially OUT OF STYLE."

All three Powerpuff Girls descended upon the two sisters and rained a shower of butt-kicking on them until the Fashionistas fled from the store.

"The evil Bikini sisters have left, but how do we undo the weird spell on Townsville?" Buttercup asked.

"I have an idea," Blossom said. "The Bikini sisters brainwashed the people of Townsville with a magazine. What if we create our own fashion magazine and re-teach Townsville how to dress?"

The Powerpuff Girls' new magazine announced the new Townsville style: wearing whatever you

want! Slowly, Townsville began to shed the layer of
Fashionista clothing it had been wearing for days,
and people put back on their old beloved garments.
Townsville was saved again!

BUBBLES GETS A PET

IT WAS a lovely spring day in Townsville, and the Powerpuff Girls just wanted to relax, eat some snacks, and watch TV. But the Professor had other ideas.

"Girls! Don't you see the sun shining? It's a beautiful day out, and you're wasting it in this dark room."

"We're not *wasting* it," Buttercup retorted. "We're watching our favorite movie, *Space Tow Truck and the Infinite Jumper Cable*. Remember the epic ending? You should watch it with us!"

"I'm sorry, but I have to put my foot down. You girls need to go outside and get some fresh air. The movie can wait until after dark. Go!" he said as he turned off the television.

The three girls reluctantly dragged themselves outside and sat down in the yard.

"We haven't even been out here a minute and I'm already bored," Blossom sighed.

"Me too," said Buttercup. "This is the worst. All I want to do is watch *Space Tow Truck and the Infinite Jumper Cable*."

Bubbles looked around as she sat next to her moping sisters. *The Professor was right*, she thought. *It is a lovely day.* Bubbles looked at the green yard and saw a beautiful butterfly flapping its wings. Bubbles suddenly realized that the yard was filled with all kinds of animals—squirrels, birds, bumblebees, chipmunks, and dragonflies. Her eyes doubled in size.

"Hey, this isn't so bad!" said Bubbles, jumping up. "Hello, Mr. Squirrel! Hello, Ms. Toad! Hello, little ants! Buzz, buzz, buzz, Mr. Bumblebee!"

Buttercup rolled her eyes. "You know animals can't understand you, right?" she said condescendingly, but Bubbles didn't hear. She had stopped in front of the great big tree in their yard. There was a little creature slowly sliding down a branch. She flew in for a closer look.

"OH MY GOSH," she gasped. "Buttercup, Blossom, come look!"

"This better be good," said Buttercup, as she and Blossom crossed the yard.

"It's a *snail*!" Bubbles squealed. "Oh my goodness, you are so adorable," Bubbles said to the snail. Its shell was a beautiful, perfect swirl and it had two adorable feelers on its head. The snail raised its head toward Bubbles. Giant hearts formed in Bubbles's eyes. She gently picked up the small creature. "I've always wanted a pet," she declared.

"Ew," said Buttercup. "Why would you want a slimy snail for a pet?"

"Yeah, Bubbles," Blossom added. "You don't even like bugs."

"This is different. He's cute!" Bubbles explained. "I'm going to call him Mr. Shelly." She flew inside to show the Professor.

"Keeping this snail is a good way to learn responsibility," the Professor said. "But you're going to need to make a terrarium for him to live in."

"A terr-ar-i-um?" Bubbles repeated. "What's that?"

"A terrarium is a miniature version of an animal's natural home in a container," the

Professor explained. "We can make one in the lab."

When they had finished building the terrarium, Bubbles gently put the snail inside.

"Welcome to your new home, Mr. Shelly!" Bubbles squealed. Mr. Shelly slowly noshed on a piece of carrot. "We are going to have a great life together!"

Meanwhile, across town, Man-Boy, the notoriously evil villain, was up to no good. Though Man-Boy had the body of a young boy, he possessed the strength of grown man. He was one of the Powerpuff Girls' worst enemies. The lovely weather had given him an idea for a new way to terrorize Townsville.

"I'm going to use my manly ax to chop down every lovely, leafy tree in Townsville. Then I'll use them to make a **MANLY ARMY OF MANLY ROBOTS!**" He laughed

maniacally. Just thinking about his manly scheme made Man-Boy so excited that his long, manly beard grew three inches.

He grabbed his ax, walked outside, and began chopping away at the first tree he saw. When it hit the ground, hundreds of birds and squirrels and butterflies scurried out of the tree. Man-Boy continued on, making his way through Townsville, destroying trees for his wooden robot army.

Eventually he made it to Town Hall, which had a beautiful lawn covered in tall trees. Man-Boy began chopping, but when the first tree went down, it fell right into the Mayor's office.

"OH NO!" the Mayor screamed, jumping up from his daily afternoon nap. "There's a tree in my office! How am I going to get my nap, I mean, uh, my work done now?" A flock of birds perched on his desk, and animals and bugs from the tree began crawling around on the floor. The Mayor went straight for his phone.

Blossom was still in the yard, bored out of her mind, when she saw her phone ringing. Blossom answered straightaway, hoping for an excuse to go back inside.

"Girls! I need your help!" the Mayor shouted over loud chirping noises.

"Mayor? Where are you? Why does it sound like you're in a forest?" Blossom asked.

"There's some young man with a very long beard cutting down all the trees in Townsville. He's threatening to destroy the entire town with wooden robots!"

"Man-Boy!" Blossom realized right away. "We'll be right there, Mayor." She hung up the phone. "Bubbles, Buttercup—the Mayor needs us. Man-Boy is terrorizing Townsville again!"

"Let's go!" Buttercup said. She and Blossom jumped up, but Bubbles lagged behind.

"Come on, Bubbles, what gives?" Blossom asked.

"I don't know, you guys," Bubbles said, looking over at her terrarium. "I think I need to stay here and take care of Mr. Shelly."

"Bubbles, he's just a snail. He'll be fine on his own. Townsville *needs* us. That's way more important than Mr. Smelly Shelly," Buttercup said.

"He's not *just* a snail," Bubbles cried. "And he's not smelly. He's my pet and my friend and I will stay here and take care of him. HE NEEDS ME!"

Blossom and Buttercup had no choice but to leave Bubbles behind. They flew to Town Hall, and Bubbles stayed home to watch over Mr. Shelly.

"Don't listen to them," Bubbles said to the snail. "You are a very special pet, and my cutest friend in the whole world."

A few hours passed, and eventually Blossom and Buttercup returned home. They had giant smiles on their faces and were out of breath, but excited.

"We totally kicked Man-Boy's butt!" Buttercup announced as she walked up to Bubbles.

"You should have been there, Bubbles," Blossom added. "It was so fun. First, Buttercup came up behind him and totally surprised him. She grabbed his ax and chopped off his beard with one swing."

"Then Blossom went like THIS, and THIS," Buttercup illustrated, punching left and right. Bubbles frowned. That *did* sound like a lot of fun, she thought. But she didn't admit it out loud.

"Mr. Shelly and I had fun, too," she insisted. "We, uh, watched the grass grow, and Mr. Shelly ate a *whole* piece of lettuce." She couldn't even think of anything to make up that sounded half as fun.

Blossom and Buttercup ignored Bubbles, and kept talking about all the fun they had saving Townsville from Man-Boy.

"Wow. Sounds great," Bubbles said sadly.

Unfortunately, Man-Boy hadn't given up on his wooden robot army yet. He knew he needed to chop down trees faster to beat the Powerpuff Girls, so he stayed up late, crafting an even manlier ax. With it, he could destroy all the trees in Townsville.

The next morning, Man-Boy set out on another path of destruction with his new ax. He cut down tree after tree, until he reached Town Hall once more. The mayor still had a gaping hole in his office, thanks to the tree that had fallen on it the day before. So when the Mayor saw Man-Boy approaching, followed by a crowd of wooden robots, he frantically called the Powerpuff Girls again.

Just like the previous day, Blossom answered the phone and told the Mayor they would be there as soon as possible.

"Bubbles, are you coming?" she asked as she and Buttercup set out to fight Man-Boy again. Bubbles looked at Mr. Shelly and paused. She wasn't sure what to do. On the one hand, she really wanted to help Buttercup and Blossom beat Man-Boy. It was no fun being left out of all the cool saving-the-day stories. On the other hand . . .

Bubbles looked at Mr. Shelly in his terrarium. He'd be

fine for just a little while, wouldn't he? Bubbles decided to go with her sisters. But as she was about to leave, Bubbles looked back and saw Mr. Shelly pressing his tiny snail face against the glass wall of the terrarium.

"NO! I can't leave him here all by himself!" she wailed, flying back over and cuddling the terrarium close to

her chest. "I'm sorry, but you'll have to fight Man-Boy without me again."

Blossom and Buttercup didn't have time to tell Bubbles how silly she was being. They just shrugged and rushed back to Town Hall.

Even though Man-Boy's new ax was ten times as big as the old one, Blossom and Buttercup weren't afraid. Buttercup rushed up to Man-Boy and pulled the ax right out of his hand, but the weight was too much for her to carry, and the ax fell to the ground, dragging Buttercup down with it.

"Aw, is my big *manly* ax too big and heavy for a little girl to carry? Don't worry, princess, swinging an ax is a man's job," he taunted her.

Buttercup fumed. She hated being called names, especially "PRINCESS." She flew up and hit Man-Boy square in the jaw. He wobbled, but quickly regained his balance and picked up the heavy ax from the ground.

"What are we going to do?" Blossom asked

Buttercup. "With his new ax, Man-Boy is too strong. We'll never be able to save Townsville without Bubbles."

But the girls had no choice but to keep fighting. They followed Man-Boy all over Townsville, doing their best to slow down his chopping and take out his robots. Man-Boy eventually chopped his way to the neighborhood where Bubbles, Buttercup, and Blossom lived.

Bubbles was inside playing with her pet snail, feeding him snacks and decorating his home. Suddenly, she heard a commotion outside.

From the window, she saw Blossom and Buttercup doing their best against Man-Boy's mighty ax. Bubbles felt guilty. She could see her sisters needed help, and there she was, refusing to join the fight.

"I'm sorry, Mr. Shelly," she said. "I will watch over you later. I need to go help defeat Man-Boy!" She hurriedly plopped Mr. Shelly back in his terrarium and flew out to join her sisters.

"Finally!" shouted Buttercup when she saw Bubbles. "We really need your help! Man-Boy's new ax is taking out every tree in Townsville."

Bubbles was ready to fight. The three Powerpuff Girls needed to work together if they were going to be able to take the giant ax from Man-Boy once and for all.

"One, two, three!" Bubbles, Blossom, and Buttercup kicked simultaneously, and their combined forces knocked Man-Boy onto his butt. While he was down, they surrounded him, and together they lifted the ax out of his hand.

The Powerpuff Girls were about to toss the ax as far as they could into oblivion. But just as they heaved back, they heard a piercing, high-pitched shriek.

"EW EW EW EW!" the voice screeched. The Powerpuff Girls looked around to see what was making the racket. They looked down, and saw something surprising: It was Man-Boy!

"Dude, what are you screaming about?" Buttercup

asked. Man-Boy was shaking. He pointed at a tiny dot on the ground next to him. The girls scratched their heads and flew in for a closer look.

"Mr. Shelly!" Bubbles exclaimed. The dot was Bubbles's sweet, harmless pet snail. "Did you follow me out here?" she asked. Gently, she picked up Mr. Shelly and flew closer to Man-Boy. "Nothing to be afraid of. It's just my snail," she said, holding the creature up to his face.

"Gross!" he said. His face went green, and it looked like he might be sick.

"Are you really afraid of a little snail?" Buttercup asked him.

"I'm not afraid! Being scared isn't manly! I just . . . I just . . ." Man-Boy took another look at the snail and burst into tears. "It's just so slimy and creepy!" he wailed, running away quickly in fear and shame.

"Well, that was easy," Blossom said. "Guess that Mr. Shelly isn't such a bad pet after all."

Bubbles looked at her pet, happy that he had managed to be so helpful.

"You're right, Blossom," Bubbles said. "But maybe I'm not quite ready to care for a pet yet." She placed the snail back on the tree exactly where she had found him.

"If you survived on your own before, you'll be fine without me now," Bubbles reassured Mr. Shelly, who had already begun to climb back up the tree. A single tear fell down her cheek as she watched him disappear into the leaves. "I'll be sure to visit you!"

Bubbles was sad, but relieved. She didn't realize how much work even a small pet would be. Now she could focus on having fun and fighting villains. She went inside with Buttercup and Blossom, and the three girls sat on the couch, finally ready to watch *Space Tow Truck and the Infinite Jumper Cable* again. They had earned a little relaxation.

BUTTERCUP AND THE SCIENCE FAIR

"**LISTEN UP,** students!" Ms. Keane said to the class. "I have an important announcement to make."

"Oooooh, is it a wonderful, magical field trip to the zoo?" asked Bubbles.

"Please tell me summer break is coming early this year," said Buttercup.

"No, no," said Ms. Keane, "nothing like that. It's time for the **ANNUAL SCIENCE FAIR!** The fair is in one week, and all students will be required to participate for a grade. I can't wait to see what kinds of projects you all come up with!"

"Yes! This is the best news ever." Blossom squealed in excitement while the rest of the class groaned. She had already thought of eight different excellent ideas for her project, and she couldn't wait to get another A+ on her report card.

Buttercup wasn't as thrilled.

"Great, extra work," she said sarcastically. She couldn't have cared less about the contest. Extra homework meant less time playing video games after school.

But then, right before class was dismissed, as the girls were gathering their books and getting ready to head home, Ms. Keane added a very important detail about this year's science fair.

"Oh! I almost forgot to mention," she said to the class. "Whoever wins first place at this year's science fair gets to be the MAYOR OF TOWNSVILLE for an entire day. Now, doesn't that sound fun?"

"Oooh," Bubbles said, her eyes growing huge.

Blossom smiled and clapped her hands in excitement. She had won the science fair every year before, and was certain this year would be no different. She could already imagine herself in charge as the mayor of Townsville. She immediately began listing all the ways she could make Townsville cleaner and better organized. She was super excited to get working on her project.

Buttercup, though, had not realized the science fair winner would get a prize at all, and was shocked by the news. She could get used to the idea of being mayor for a day. Buttercup had some pretty great ideas of what she would do if she were in charge—and they were nothing like Blossom's plans. Her first action would be to ban the word *princess* and get rid of all the girly stuff in Townsville. Buttercup decided she was going to win that prize herself.

When she got home that afternoon, Buttercup tried to come up with an idea for a project that could win the

science fair. Blossom already knew exactly what she was going to do, and she was beaming with pride.

"I'm going to conduct a molecular analysis of Chemical X, and test the effects it has on different plants," she told her sisters. She knew it would be more complicated and advanced, and therefore a lot more impressive, than any of the projects her classmates were doing. Buttercup had to admit, it was a pretty good idea and would be tough to beat.

Bubbles was excited about her idea for a science fair project, too.

"I'm going to do a project about UNICORNS!" she exclaimed.

"But, Bubbles," Blossom said, "unicorns aren't even real."

"Yes, they are!" Bubbles insisted. "And I'm going to use my project to prove it. I'm going to collect evidence from all over Townsville and use it to prove to everyone that unicorns really do exist."

"Good luck with that one," Buttercup said, smirking.

Blossom thought Bubbles's idea wasn't great, but didn't say anything else to her since she wanted to win. "What about you, Buttercup? What's your science fair project going to be about?"

Buttercup sighed. She had been thinking about the science fair all afternoon and still had no idea what she was going to do for her project. But she really wanted to be in charge of Townsville for a day (especially since Blossom, the leader of the Powerpuff Girls, already got to be the boss all of the time). She was determined to come up with a winning idea.

Thinking about it after dinner, Buttercup remembered that the Professor was a scientist. He conducted scientific experiments all the time in his lab.

Maybe if I go to the Professor's lab, I'll find some ideas for my project there, she thought. She ventured down to his lab and looked through all of the Professor's tools and equipment, hoping to find some inspiration. Buttercup wandered around and looked at the Professor's beakers, jars, and microscopes, but she didn't find anything in the lab that she thought would make a good science fair project—especially one that would be better than Blossom's.

Buttercup went back to the living room and sat on the couch. She crossed her arms in frustration. The

Professor found her moping there, and he asked her what was wrong.

"This science fair is so stupid," she said. "I really want to win, but I can't think of anything that will make a good project."

"Well, Buttercup, like any good scientist, you need to find a topic that interests you. Study something you care about," the Professor advised.

"Huh," Buttercup wondered aloud. "I guess my favorite things are kicking butt and fighting villains, but there's no way I can make a science fair project out of that," she said.

"Sure you can!" the Professor exclaimed. "Science is everywhere. All we have to do is think of a way it relates to, as you put it, kicking butt. I know you'll come up with something great."

That night, Buttercup stayed up late and brainstormed all kinds of ideas for her science fair project. Finally, she came up with the perfect plan.

When Blossom and Bubbles woke up the next morning, Buttercup was already out of bed. They found her in the living room, hard at work hammering and sawing. She was building some kind of strange contraption.

"Buttercup, what are you doing?" Bubbles asked, rubbing her eyes tiredly.

"I'm building a catapult for the science fair. It's a kind of weapon that lets you fling objects really far. You've gotta use some heavy science, like physics, to make it work. And the better you build it, the farther you can fling stuff. You can use it to launch ammo and TOTALLY KICK BUTT!" she told her sisters with excitement. "My catapult will be so big and powerful that my science fair project will break a world record for strongest catapult

throw of all time. That way I'll definitely win the science fair."

Blossom didn't want to admit it, but Buttercup's catapult was looking pretty cool . . . and pretty scientific, too.

At school, Buttercup went to the library and checked out a few books about catapults and physics and read them at lunch, in the hall, and during class.

"Wow, Buttercup, I've never seen you study so much," Ms. Keane observed. Buttercup just nodded and kept reading. If her project was going to win the science fair, it had to be perfect.

Bubbles and Blossom were also working hard on their projects. Bubbles was learning a lot about unicorns, and had gathered some good evidence that could prove they were real. So far, she had a few shiny hairs that looked like they *might* come from a unicorn's tail, as well as some blurry photographs that, if you squinted your left eye a bit, looked like they *might* be pictures of unicorns.

Blossom had managed to test CHEMICAL X on a lot of different kinds of plants, and had seen some weird mutations taking place a result. One rose's thorns had grown twice as sharp after being exposed to Chemical X, and the flowers could now fly off the stems like helicopters. A small blade of grass Blossom had dipped into a jar of Chemical X sprouted up in size so quickly that it was soon as big as a tree.

A week went by, and it was finally the day of the science fair. All three Powerpuff Girls proudly took their projects to the school to display. Blossom and Buttercup each hoped theirs would win the coveted prize. (Bubbles didn't care about the prize; she just wanted to show people that unicorns were real and amazing.)

The science fair projects were ready to be judged by Ms. Keane and, of course, the actual Mayor of Townsville. As they walked around the cafeteria, the girls waited next to their displays. While they were waiting, a familiar but unwelcome face appeared: Princess Morbucks.

"Hello, **POWERPUFF GIRLS**, I hope you're all ready to lose the science fair," she said, holding up her project: a giant model of a volcano.

"No way," said Blossom with a laugh, looking at what Princess Morbucks had brought to school. "Volcano science fair projects are *so* unoriginal. I did one just like that years ago. There's no way that will win the prize."

"Yeah, dude, your project is so sad," Buttercup added confidently.

"Well, my volcano is different," Princess Morbucks explained. "First of all, it's made from *actual* volcanic rocks, and it has super special high-tech lights that make it glow. Plus, it's hooked up to my phone, so all I have to do to make it erupt like a volcano is press this button." She showed the Powerpuff Girls the button on her phone's screen. "It was really expensive, so there's

no way anyone but me, the RICHEST GIRL IN TOWNSVILLE, could afford it."

"You're not supposed to *buy* your science fair project," Bubbles told Princess Morbucks. "You're supposed to make it yourself. Otherwise it's cheating."

"More importantly, you won't learn anything about science," Blossom said. "That's kind of the whole point."

Princess Morbucks rolled her eyes and walked away to go set up her volcano across the room. The Powerpuff Girls knew Princess Morbucks's project had no chance of winning. What they didn't know, however, was that her volcano actually had another special power.

"I *will* win," Princess Morbucks grumbled to herself. "Because when I control the volcano with my phone, I'll kick the eruption into overdrive. Then, when it explodes, everyone's projects will be destroyed, and they'll be forced to crown me the winner of the science fair. And when I'm mayor of Townsville, I'll make a decree that I, Princess Morbucks, am an official Powerpuff Girl! And then I'll take away Bubbles, Blossom, and Buttercup's powers so that I am the ONE AND ONLY POWERPUFF GIRL in all of Townsville!"

Just then, Princess Morbucks saw that Ms. Keane and the Mayor of Townsville were approaching the Powerpuff Girls' projects to judge them for the fair, and she got ready to set off her destructive volcano.

Meanwhile, the girls were getting ready for their presentations. Blossom was rearranging her tray of mutant plants, and Bubbles was combing her unicorn hairs. Buttercup set up her catapult and got it into launching position for when the judges came by.

Ms. Keane and the Mayor walked up to Buttercup, and began to look at her project.

"Wow, that is a very large catapult," the Mayor said, and checked off a box on his score sheet.

Buttercup explained some of the science stuff that she'd studied, then told them that she planned to use her catapult to launch the largest rock the farthest distance ever recorded.

"Very ambitious, Buttercup!" said Ms. Keane as she wrote something down. Buttercup loaded a giant rock into the catapult.

Meanwhile, Princess Morbucks was about to press the button on her phone that would unleash a torrent of lava to destroy all the other projects at the science fair and make her the winner by default.

As Buttercup launched her catapult, Princess Morbucks moved her finger to the button. Everyone in the cafeteria gasped as they watched Buttercup's rock fly across the cafeteria. How far would it go? The rock came down and landed—right inside the hole at the top of Princess Morbucks's volcano.

Princess Morbucks pressed the button for the

volcano to explode, but now that Buttercup's rock was lodged inside, the dangerous lava couldn't get out. The high-tech volcano completely malfunctioned—it sputtered, and its special lights flickered and went dark.

Princess Morbucks was furious. "Why did I spend so much money on this stupid volcano if it doesn't even work?" she asked angrily and kicked the broken volcanic model. "Stupid, stupid, worthless volcano!" she said, kicking harder. Suddenly the volcano turned back on. The lights flashed brightly, and the added force of Princess Morbucks's kick jolted Buttercup's rock and knocked it out of the volcano. The lava finally EXPLODED out of the volcano, and soon the entire cafeteria was covered in the hot goop. Just as Princess Morbucks had hoped, all of the science fair projects were now covered in lava. Including her own.

But all was not lost for Buttercup. Even though her catapult was now gunked up with a lot of expensive fake lava, the judges decided they'd scored enough

of the projects to make a decision. And since Princess
Morbucks didn't wait her turn before she launched her
volcano and destroyed everything, the judges decided
they couldn't give her a grade. They were the most
impressed with Buttercup's use of advanced physics,
and agreed that the rock had gone farther than any

other catapulted rock they'd ever seen. Buttercup was declared the winner. Even Blossom agreed she deserved it.

The next Monday, Buttercup got to spend the whole day being the mayor of Townsville. Her first decree was that, while she was in charge, **NO GIRLY STUFF** was allowed, and no one was allowed to say the word *princess*.

Especially "Princess" Morbucks.